FINDING THE NAME

AN ANTHOLOGY

EDITED BY
ELISAVIETTA RITCHIE

FINDING THE NAME

an anthology of poems by

E. Castendyk Briefs
Maxine Combs
Lucia Dunham
Elizabeth Follin-Jones
Barbara Goldberg
Elaine Reisler Magarrell
Mariquita MacManus Mullan
Elisavietta Ritchie
Elizabeth Sullam
Margaret Weaver

THE WINEBERRY PRESS

1983

Illustrations by Elizabeth Follin-Jones
Typography by Kathryn E. King

Library of Congress Card Number: 83-62225
ISBN: 0-9612158-0-1

THE WINEBERRY PRESS

c/o The Writer's Center
P.O. Box 606
Glen Echo, Maryland 20812

EDITOR'S NOTE

When the ceiling crumbled over the bookstall classroom at the old Writer's Center in Glen Echo, Maryland, we moved our workshops to my living room in Washington, D.C. These "master classes" ebbed and flowed with the seasons. Invitations to publish and to give readings began to come in. Finally nine of the participants and I collaborated on this anthology, and the Wineberry Press was born.

Elisavietta Ritchie

ACKNOWLEDGMENTS

The authors wish to thank the publications which have also accepted some of the poems in this anthology. Unless otherwise noted, the copyright is held by the individual author, to whom reprint rights have reverted, and by whom permission has been granted to publish the poems in this collection.

E. Castendyk Briefs: "Alzheimer's at Bill and Sally's," © *The American Poetry Anthology.* "The Sitting." © *The Christian Science Monitor.* "Montmartre Stairway," © *The New Yorker.*

Maxine Combs: "Prescription," © *Piedmont Literary Review.* "February 11, 1983," *Tide Turning: An Anthology of Poems on the Endangered Marine Species.* "Old Remedies," *Whose Woods These Are.*

Elizabeth Follin-Jones: "Cold Rain," *Operative.* "In The Singular," *Whose Woods These Are.*

Barbara Goldberg: "Moorings," *As Is.* "Journal entry, All Saints' Day, 1427," *Nimrod.* "Song While Arranging Jasmine and Jewelweed," *Tendril.* "Nee Maggie Malone," *Whose Woods These Are.* "Cultivated Ground," *Poetry Now.* "Teeth" and "Cautionary Tales," *Poetry.* "Coming of Age," *Washington Review.*

Elaine Magarrell: "On Hogback Mountain," *Poet Lore.*

Mariquita MacManus Mullan: "Incident at Dow," *Piedmont Literary Review.* "Mirage" and "The Professor," © *Christian Science Monitor.* "Stopped For A Red Light: Miami," *Whose Woods These Are.* "Memorial Day On Omaha Beach," *The Archer.*

Elisavietta Ritchie: "The Gypsy Is Summoned Before The Militia" and "For A Certain Slavic Novelist," *Whose Woods These Are.* "In The Archives," reprinted by permission of the Poetry Society of America. Originally published in *The Poetry Review* (or other PSA publication), Vol. 1, No. 1, fall/spring 1983. Copyright © 1983 by Elisavietta Ritchie. "My Father, Colonel U.S. Army, Retired," *New CollAge.* "Sisterhood," *Women: A Journal of Liberation* and *A Sheath Of Dreams And Other Games.* "Propitiations," *Poetry Society of Georgia's Anthology of Prizewinning Poems.* "Homecoming From Indonesia," *Visions.* "Choreography," earlier versions in *Salome* and *Moving To Larger Quarters;* also performed as theater piece in The Poem Is The Last Resort, created and directed by Jerilyn Gilstrap. "The Nantucket Whaler's Lady," *The Nauset Calendar* and *Poetry Engagement Book 1984.* "Learning To Keep a Low Profile," earlier versions in *Washingtonian Magazine, The Poet Upstairs* and *Operative.*

Elizabeth Sullam: "Mine Field" and "August In The Emilian Lowlands," *Federal Poets.*

Margaret Weaver: "Lullaby" and "The Hawk," *Poet Lore.* "Orange," *Passages North.* "Revenant," *Kyriokos.* "The Vineyard," *Kavitha.* "Collected Fairy Tales," *Taurus.* "Stranded Whales," *Tide Turning: An Anthology of Poems on the Endangered Marine Species.* "Under Water," reprinted with permission from the August 1982 issue of *Yankee* magazine, Yankee Publishing Inc., Dublin, NH 03444. © 1982.

TABLE OF CONTENTS

E. Castendyk Briefs

NAMINGS

Now West owes fewer names to totem, hero, ancestor
or saint; the East to iron rice pot, bird, bamboo —
whatever fixed a birthing mother's eye.

North still knows Eskimos who bid their naming-crone
to births: venerable reel of names shrilly unwinding
for the infant on its way.

Sharp listener in the womb, he waits for the sounds
he knows his own. When they strike, he flings himself upon them, and with a yell, roughrides his name
into the world.

BIDU SAYAO, SOPRANO

Bidu Sayao, Sayao, Bidu,
name chanting the rainforest's
daylong twilight; diver's gloom
streaked by feathers
vivid as tropical fish.

Bidu, Bidu Sayao, Bidu —
the syllables glide
from birdcall to sob,
from threat to promises of power
confirmed in neon golds and greens.

Earth name, itself a singing,
climbing, briefly free;
sunbird captured by sky,
recaptured by dark clods:
Bidu Sayao

OLD-HAWAIIAN DEATH ON THE BIG ISLAND

When Mele died, the Territory mourned.
Kamehameha blood runs rare, and when it stops,
the grief is a splendid thing.

Mele always rested afternoons
on the curving, broad lanai
screened by tree fern and torch ginger.
The train of her linen *holoku*
spilled a daily rainpool on the floor.

That day it rippled silk. Her jewels,
rope-like leis of rarest yellow down
stitched thick and smooth as on live feathered breast:
royalty's due from royal O-o bird.
That day she did not sleep alone
but in a grove of women straight
as the man-high *kahili* each one held
to sway the flowered air.

All day and long into the night, solemn throats intoned
a voyage chant lonely, austere,
No one would tell me what the dark words knew.

FAT MAMA IN LOUIS' ICE-CREAM PARLOUR

Like the wife of the full moon, she rolls
through groping philodendron leaves
to the last terrace table, daughter
moon in the first quarter trailing after.

Or like vanilla roses: one
slowly melting, overblown,
one — from the same cutting — tapered bud
crisp from its mold.

Face and facsimile stamped young.
On daughter's features I can trace
old beauties of the given bone
buried in mama's fleshful ruin.

Behind my leaves I sip and spy.
How rapidly their double sundae specials
disappear! At every mouthful I
grow heavier.

ALZHEIMER'S AT BILL AND SALLY'S

"Who was the nice young lady in my bed?"
Bill whispers to me at the breakfast table.

"Probably Sal," I breathe back, "your wife."
Relieved, Bill laughs — his old good laugh, "That's rich!"

Grateful for any joke, Sally joins in, then throws me
her four-children-and-thirty-years look . . . .

Bill jerks away from his breakfast nap,
checks his tie, gets up, and with a cheerful

"Good night!" heads for his room. Always courtly,
at the stairs he turns, almost bows to Sally,

"Miss, will I see you yesterday?"
Sally waves, tired. Bill stands waiting.

Of course you will, dear William,
who loved her twice as much tomorrow.

THE SITTING

Glimpses of white against the dark of trees as I drove past the niche of sassafras and black walnut, where the horseshoe east of Snicker's Gap straightens into Bluemont.

On the way back I slowed: large patch of beard, clean white sweatshirt, mane; small twists of the same hirsute white like pulled-up awnings over caves of eyes; and well beyond the boulder the man sat on, crossed white canvas feet.

What features I could spy in all that combed white fall were unremarkable and still as river stones.

Whenever I drove to Bluemont at five-thirty, he was there. I took to nodding as I passed. Barely, he acknowledged me and instantly resumed his vigil. Who was he; what was it he expected from that fold in the oldest mountains?

At last I asked at the village store.

"William Jason Dapplewood, that's who, and what he's waiting for's plain. History to be corrected, guess he'd call it. Year back, he was walking home from work unkempt, painty overall, when some slick with a District tag snapped his likeness and took off. Newspaper man he thinks. Bothered him no end. Since, he's waited every evening that was fair."

"What on earth for?"

"To have his other picture taken, ma'am, for the record, that's what, for the record to be whole."

MONTMARTRE STAIRWAY

Down
We stepped,
Three-legged as
A lover tango pair,
Lightly as wingless angels
Might proceed on mottled air,
Moving on silent feet from cloud
To cloud — half walking and half blown.
Below, a darkened city slept and watched
The pale unravelling of her stream, while we,
Sleepwalkers, floated down, one shadow in a plated dream,
Till, dizzied by a height that neither stair nor hill had known,
We reeled, eyes closed, who'd reached the bottom step but one.

SUMMER EVENING IN THE SALZKAMMERGUT

You left me the brown bees in these lindens
dark with age and the hour at lake's edge.
Heavy on the skin the lindened air.
No breath of wind or word. Stir
only of bee-work and mirrored mountains
wrinkling under waterstriders' feet.
When out of the dusk a leapt fish whitely crashes,
shattered summits quickly mend.

Hard mountain peace mends disparate things:
rips in the broad-loomed quiet,
peak-slashed cloud,
the jagged cleft in faith.
If not soon, later it will mend
what your words tore.

INTO WINTER

Autumn-sated eye rests now
as color cedes to form,
senses grope for deeper sense.

World folds itself away.
I unfold toward the blank page
of winter's rich austerity,

hold pencil-still and wait
for the blade that winter whets
to sharpen me.

ALL HALLOW'S

Mountain-high moon.
Straight out of Ezekiel
it comes,
this lustre of a world carved
from risen, dazzlewhite bone.

TWO FROM CISTERCIAN WHITE

Holy Cross Abbey, Berryville, Virginia

I. Trappist Silence

Angel, speak louder, I'm hard of hearing
and love the shudder of your voice, though stern.

Above the pounding quiet I make out
a phrase, but plainer, please.

Roll meaning straight as dew down grassy spine,
down mine.

II. "Thou fool, that which thou sowest is not quickened except it die." Cor. 15:36

Once tall, now curved like a bishop's crosier,
once quick, now pushing swollen sandals
over the polished black and white linoleum,
two monks shuffle toward their place
among hale chanting brothers.

A process by inches, but they make it
in time for the Our Father and His Bread.
Bright in the stubble of grey faces,
flickers of the light they're closest to:
pair of old Trappists gone to seed.

Maxine Combs

LAMENT

Hear the lament of cat-headed Sekhet
Offered now neither reseeding fruits,
Nor amulets hacked from the flesh of sea rams;

The dirge for Serapis,
Dog at his feet, crowned by a falcon,
Neglected in priestly processions,
Excised from pillars.

Shadows of a broken lyre.

READING RIMBAUD

How pale eyed birds
Above a sobbing sea
Flew towards
Dorado;

How a fiery sun,
In birdless space,
Pressed down the eyelids
Of the sea;

How the color of love
Is bitter red.

DREAM POEM

In my last night's dream
I stared into a mirror framed on three sides
And saw a young girl wrapping her head in red thread.

Then, in a meadow, she trapped a swallow with a stone
    in its stomach,
Wrapped the stone in a linen handkerchief,
Stuck it under her arm.

Thus I could see how her headaches were defeated. And
    the thief
Who had stolen her heart eventually returned it.
This is the third time I've dreamed this dream.

OLD REMEDIES

One night when I lay unable to sleep,
I opened my book of Egyptian secrets
and found this prescription: anoint the pulses
    on both arms with oil of coral
and sleep will come.

Another night, lonely and coughing,
I mixed violet water, licorice, and a knife point
    of saffron
into a powder that deadened my throat and heart.

And when I needed a cure for an obscure injury,
I plaited wool flowers with white lilies, stirred in
    a thimbleful of melted beeswax,
and greased the spot.

You ask: do you really believe these old remedies
    work?
After all, we live in the twentieth century.
For answer, I pour dragon's blood into a dollar's worth
    of red wine (an old recipe for dispelling doubt)
and urge you to join me as we consider my chances.

22

PRESCRIPTION

An old prescription states:
take the ear of a black cat
boil it in the white milk
of a black cow;
wear it as a thumb cover
and you will turn invisible.

Now I dream of invisible demons,
some male, some female,
who hide near gates or nut trees,
lurk by roads,
surround us on all sides
as earth surrounds the roots of vines.

In my dream these demons cast no shadows
yet they reveal the future by
oil and eggshells.
In my dream an old woman tells me
how horses see demons
if demons are present.

She tells me how
a mule discovered silver
near Boise, Idaho,
how bees attend funerals,
fish commit suicide,
black snails cure cancer.

And in her singsong voice points out
as Spinoza pointed out
there is no difference between large and small events:
a dead fish, a man turning
invisible, a demon
seeking shade at midnight.

WINTER NIGHT

Once the four rivers of Paradise
Could be crossed dry-shod,
Fishes caught, the dead communed with,

The furniture protected
If the proper words
Were known and spoken.

Words chanted calmed the sea,
And fingers knotted winds
Stored in leather bags.

An ancient man before a hard ascent
Hurled a stone
And found renewal.

A Greek wife poured fat
On a bird's back and saw
Her bad luck fly away.

A sick boy dropped an empty bowl,
Watched a stranger kick it
And catch his fever.

Yesterday in the snow as I played
Cat's cradle, my string broke,
And the sun slid beyond my reach.

I searched for hours,
Fasted, scoured the wooden floors,
Waited, sat down, began at last

To carve the necessary arrows.
All night I labored.
A gate banged at the edge of the garden,

And once I heard footsteps
But couldn't tell if they
Were coming or going. Down the hall

A child sighed or the wind
Whistled through a flute
Scraped from a human bone.

When the final hour came,
I mixed incense with charcoal,
supplicated the knotted winds,

Dipped my arrows in fire,
Shot them straight up,
Rekindled the sun.

THE DEMON LOVER

An angel of the bizarre arrived in a dream
From the absolute elsewhere, from the parallel universe
Where the same billiard ball drops in two holes at once.

With a metal beater he struck his four-sided triangle,
And toads, embedded for centuries in stone,
Hopped out on the desert.

From Point Omega where he stood
He toasted me with Raven's Wing;
I stood transfixed in a field of gold.

He swept me away, kept me seven years
In the hollow, moonless earth. In the cold
We could see the fires of the city of Schamballah.

When the broken clock tolled, I escaped through the rocks,
Up past the red lion, past the river of crocodiles,
Following a Chaldean star map, faded by flooding.

Now down to one self, the sun on my neck,
I cross the blue gravel, the marigold fields,
Quiescent but moving, bright but not dazzling.

THE TOMB ROBBER

Tonight I feel an affinity
with a hard nomadic existence,
a tomb robber's life in seasonal times;

those imprecise days when noon was a local event,
when hours were rarely equal,
when years stretched out to different lengths,

before sundials or water clocks,
when the stars stayed fixed on the dome of a box,
and in certain years the moon eclipsed red.

These were days when prophets examined livers,
taught the transmigration of souls,
traded for amber and tin in the Baltic,

learned to make glass and then forgot how,
drew on the walls what they wanted to happen
confused plants and animals,

promised the man with the injured arm
he would meet in sleep
the god who would cure him;

forgave the stranger
who sold the golden bowls of the dead,
and bartered old bracelets for flat bread.

DRAGON PATHS

Using willow stick and pendulum,
Following underground streams,
Paths under roads,
A diviner in an old tweed coat and hiking boots
Tracked the earth force across the English hills
To the nave of a country church,
Aligned on geodetic lines,
As stone circles had been
On the same auspicious site.

The wild hare in moonlight
Knows what lies under old roads,
Under the bramble of nut blossoms, the red chalk
    stone, the castle mounds,
Knows as the palmer once knew
The old straight tracks between mountain peaks,
The hard paths through lake and bog,
Those deeper roads,
Waymarked by pillars, notches cut in ridges,
Reflected light from dew ponds, holy wells,
A planted clump of trees,
All pointing to key stones
That mapped earth and sky.

These ways are haunted by dragons and black dogs,
They guide antelopes straight across the Himalayas,
Cross and recross at centers of influence,
At times spiral like the prehistoric serpent,
Evoke the body that sleeps,
The giant veined by intersecting paths,
Forgotten in our indifferent times,
Until the diviner remembers
And comes to probe his pulse
That shudders under the altar of stone.

FEBRUARY 11, 1983

Outside it's snowing hard enough to freeze a mammoth
which reminds me that traders near the Bering Sea
include in their vocabulary

a word that means to die of cold.
They also have a word
that means to die of longing.

Those Northern people knew a thing or two
about the gravities that down the heart;
they had the time to think them through

while waiting days to sight a seal's head in sea ice,
or sitting winter nights in houses carved from snow,
months away from a different season
      and the opposite of cold.

Lucia Dunham

FROM NAPOLEON ON ST. HELENA

Not that I was unaccustomed to choices.
There was always a tangle of trails on the forest floor,
but I followed a steady road to reason. Voices
called me to build in the bloody steps of war.

My suffering France won such a state of order
as citizens can reach if leaders dare.
And I yearned for the same in countries past her border.
I rose to my zenith in Egypt, soon aware
her people loved me. My sole ambition —
to broadcast Justice when cannon did not resolve
the rights of man. I held to my reasonable mission
while eight thousand times the earth revolved
around its imagined spindle. Sure at the last
that France and the others wavered, I stood fast.

Lucia Dunham

EMPEROR QIN SHIHUANGDI BEFORE HIS LAST JOURNEY

My soldiers of clay are at their battle stations,
in ranks of solemn thousands in the earth.
You know I made the warring states a nation,
nurtured on laws and dogma from its birth.
Stone by stone, my slaves raised up The Wall;
and built this mausoleum the soldiers guard
so none may breach my tomb in the jeweled hall
laced with quicksilver rivers. *Entry barred.*

I pace the ramps and ramparts, face a swarm
of ranting ghosts of slaves, ill-clothed, ill-fed.
Once when a mountain blocked my way with storm,
I stripped its flank of trees. All wish me dead.

I note an empty garrison by the portal.
This too I must man with guards. If I am mortal.

THE BONES REPLY

You ask what use are bones. My own have grown
to royal use beneath this monument
that bears a chiseled figure on a throne
incised with the King's name. By accident,
my ordinary bones lie here instead
of his, jumbled in battle. No one sure
which bones belonged to leader, which to led,
our bones were so alike. We both endure —
the King, without the bones that had his name,
sees mine serve well to uphold his fiery fame.
While I, who when others speak of deeds, am dumb,
prosper on sunny days when people come
to honor these mistaken bones which pull
kingly memories that are bountiful.

RUMORS OF WAR

Under the flowing torches,
through rows of shattered glass,
children and their shadows
rummage for loot.

The boy with hands cuffed behind,
measures as best he can
his rhythmic step
between two hurrying men.

Youths weave their sinister ballet
among the cars and buses,
leap through banners of smoke,
brandish fire. Whirl and shoot.

And over the mountains,
across water or around the corner,
hordes of children
follow the arcs of flung stones.

THE MARCHERS

Once the beaten
parade ground shook
beneath their feet

Colors wheeled
Challenges rang out
Trumpets flashed stars

Now their voices
are wrapped in wind
their shadows drift down-sky

RACE IN THE ORCHARD

Pickers still reach up and over the branches
twisting and plucking handily to the pails
that pull on their shoulders, numb yet limbering.
Apples roll in the bins, light fails,
and bone-weary pickers clamber on the buses.

Sunset glows and dusk flows to trees,
whitens foreshortened ladders propped for night.
Two boys swing into the grove on forklift trucks;
one lifts a bin and whirrs in the half-light,
up-lane, to unload by the trucking loop at the end.

There in the evening cold, rectangular bins
huddle, as apples exhale warmth from the sun.
Dollops of fragrance gone by morning, when
the burly trucks will rumble, one by one,
to shoulder bounty in to market.

Without his load, the boy swings back to the grove
down the rutted lane, and where it widens midway,
he meets and passes the other rider coming.
Both are whipped to haste by the waning day,
their hair streams, faces glitter.

The pace quickens. One sweeps by with apples,
the other returns without, at breakneck speed;
lift, hail and pass, unload, return
always meeting at midpoint as if freed
to travel faster but not lose the pattern.

Hurry. Flight is the order of evening.
These are angels-possessed, they cleave the air
in a race that is steady, deliberate, swift —
but there is no winner here with streaming hair,
only, speed of the race outstripping nightfall.

Lucia Dunham

OXFORD-MONROE APARTMENTS

A path crosses the square lot through weeds
sprawled over a frost-bitten garden,
where the seven-storied Oxford-Monroe
bustled with people for eighty years.

I recall gray limestone and the massive sills.
Floor tiles were cracked in the dank hall,
metallic stairs woke echoes.
You jangled the bell for a rattling cage
and a crooked man wet with mop and pail,
beckoned to follow, clanged the gates,
pulled the cable. The cage bumped, hesitated.

A smell of cabbage and gravy flowed from apartments,
ample Victorian — now divided for student, artist,
alien, the uncertain old. Here, half a parlor,
there, kitchen and servant's room thrown together;
beyond, a cluster of bedrooms and bath in a pantry.
Furniture came from student exchange by the tracks,
knickknacks from the five-and-dime.

That year the two girls, Economics and Sociology,
slept in a fever of passion with the man next door —
Economics one Saturday, Sociology the next,
and anxiously petitioned the moon.
The young philosopher found himself charmed, bedeviled.
Across the hall, a hunter of man-eating tigers,
wanting the jungle, blunted his loss in gin rickeys.

The artist here was bemused by Beauty
though the colors coiled on her palette
would not transform to the magical scenes
she had glimpsed from windows within.
And the old couple doddered day-long,
bluffly decrepit, yet reached at night,
each to the other's warmth.

I am still on the street near this gap
at the end of a city block full
of the sunset, blotted out when
shadows move in and street lamps flare.

HOMING FLIGHT

Seated in rows, sheltered
in this airworthy cocoon
as it dips through
layers of cloud,
suddenly we come
to wider light,
and drift on level course,
suspended
above a countryside
where only autos
glint in passage.

Men's markings lie over the land:
geometric fields of green, brown, tan,
a farmhouse, barn, and faintly —
motionless wooden cows;
streets of a narrow town,
a flat-topped school.
Nowhere
man, woman, or child.

It seems when flying over,
the erect fragile earthbound people
are undiscovered as blades of grass.

Now droning through a dream,
we glide along the confines
where lightly swaying buildings
bloom upward to our plane.
Like hard rectangular flowers,
not planted by our kinsmen
but growing of themselves,
needing time only
to reach so high.

The plane purrs loudly,
banks to a turn and long descent
over the lower town,
skims a finger of water,
brushes the runway
and with bump and hum,
rolls to a stop
on the gunmetal tarmac.

We set our feet in port,
the trysting place. Changelings
among the people we conjured,
the unseen blades of grass.

HAUNTED MUSEUM

Their hands hover like birds
whistled in by the passion of works
that will not let them go.
The magnificent dead artists return.

The hands of a sculptor shape the air,
finger a hooded robe, smooth a cheek
in bronze. The painters' hands
swoop unfaltering to pools, forests

and marigolds of color,
wing home in season as the birds do.
Quicken the portrait faces —
gaunt, merry, in reverie.

And hands of a potter
without a name, touch and circle
circle and touch, a ruddy bowl
scored with crab and eagle.

Time and again we tingle
with the turning, whispering, humming
presence of hands that dart and wheel
about us like flurries of birds.

SQUIRREL

You arch your body
in flowing leaps.
You astonish me.
You will go on forever.

A car sweeps the road
leaves you suddenly
ruffled, limp,
mortal.

And the passage in your life
we shared
can mean no more to me now
than a meteor I once saw

pierce the sky
and plunge back to dark
before I knew it came.

Elizabeth Follin-Jones

TALKING WITH MARY

Mary would agree — endings
are untidy, beginnings unmarked.
Friends overlap lovers,
casual words may spark a storm.

In Denver we wrestled
with Sartre and Spock,
bartered opinions over coffee,
and cradled beginnings.

Our words spill now
through two thousand miles,
ghost unwritten letters, rage
for her husband dead — at fifty.

I know her impatience with fools.
Sometimes I hear the look
on her face when I'm out
on a limb. I listen to Mary.

IN THE SINGULAR

Edward believes there is no life
beyond us in the universe.
He is waving his hand for a taxi.
His eyes squint in the sun.

People converge and skirt him.
A bus sends tremors along the curb.
Dominick's waits to feed us as if
it had all the time in the world.

Edward maintains the odds of creation
repeating in space are far too remote
to consider. Sometimes he scratches
equations in dust or watches volcanos

or bets on short odds at poker. Down
on the corner two men peddle flowers.
Horns splatter their scent. A scarf
escapes from a woman riding a Vespa.

The taxi driver has blackguard eyebrows
and seven children. Edward departs
on a trip to Antarctica. We both know
that someday the sun will grow cold.

BEYOND THE LIGHTHOUSE

Atlantis rises from the sea.
Low sun through cirrus
ambers walls
spread beside the shore.
Stones piled in towers would have crumbled long ago.

High on our roof,
we ache to explore old passages,
mosaics, frescoes crusted over.
Niches.
Rooms that hold the shape of living.

Clouds flower,
leaf in wisps of fog,
deepen the island.

Dawn is a mist strewn with seaweed.
Before it drifts,
Atlantis flees our grasp.

CHRYSALIS

Anne on her knees
squints at a moth,
holds out a twig
for a June bug,
then scatters fuzz
from the cottonwood.
Anne counts
her future on daisies.

I dig plantains
from the strawberry bed,
lay down netting
to fend off slugs.
My tendrils sink
to the bottom of rocks.
I've merged
with the crop of berries.

COLD RAIN

On the day we go to the cape,
it will rain cold rain.
The edges of flowers will fray.

A button will drop from your coat
in the cab while I pause to answer the phone.
It's only your broker.

This year I'll color my hair deep red,
wear skirts that slit at the knee,
hold onto your arm in the fog

on the dunes. Walk without shadow.
Who should be told if we both get lost
on our way out to dinner?

When we come home past the houses
shut tight to the eaves,
our hedge will look seedy.

The cat next door will desert
his post under the porch to greet us.
Our mail will catch in the jam:

we've been selected to win a prize.
The dentist announces his move
to an inconvenient location.

It will be raining cold rain as it always
rains on vacation. It will next year.
So far there has always been a next year.

THE ROCKER

This Windsor chair rocks her in time, and keeps
a filament of present locked in place.
She speaks in cadenced words of loss that sleeps
beneath the timbre of its balanced pace,
yet seeps at night through dreams that crimp and make
her bed a crumpled travesty of rest.
She trims the night to hoard the hours awake,
crochets a web of day, a patchwork vest
to wrap against the chill of age, and feel
alive with light and sound and burnished pine
that cradle her in strength, and sway to heal
in motion what dark chambers undermine.

My ear is keyed to count the beat. I fill
with hurt to hear her pendulum swing still.

Elizabeth Follin-Jones

SILHOUETTES

Wintered oaks collage
against a salmon sky.
Dogwoods weave a filigree on snow.

Grandfather showed me how cedars
turn to cutouts pasted on a wall.
There's his shadow between the trunks.

My cat at the lighted pane
becomes a pattern on the glass.
I search through dusk

for Grandfather's face,
diminished now to a silhouette.

KINETICS

We waded, ice maidens, in the springhouse,
ran blue feet to the well,
drank iron from a stubborn pump.

And while Jenny and I raced hens,
climbed rough wood to the loft,
sneezed and were laced in boa webs,

Grandmother entertained ancients,
spread placid tales on teacakes,
gave her time of day.

Caught in the kitchen
and forced to tangle
our grubby hands and sprouting braids

with How do you do's, ten minutes
we listened to sages speak
of vintage wisteria and lightning bolts.

Then giggling Excuse me's, we leaped
and scraped to the top of an oak
to look at forever forever like hawks.

ELLIPSES

At first they studied the planets
because they were magic.
They had always worshipped the sun

and the magnet of stars.
Comets took the wisdom
of gods to decipher.

Planets sheltered warmth
in their orbits.
Especially Mars. And Venus

nestled the sickle Moon.
Everyone tasted
the Moon in their lives.

THE BAG LADY

clings like a clone.
I stuff her sack with rags,
hide it under my cashmere coat.

I wash my hair. Beneath
these curls, dirty strands
grip my neck.

Look inside my kidskin pumps.
Socks glue to scuffs
lined with cardboard and sweat.

Today I slept
on the post office radiator.
Heat climbed into my bones.

But let some bum sprawl on my grate,
I'll shove him off.
No one is pushing me around.

Here among my tailored friends,
you do not smell my chianti dregs,
or feel my sinews

tensed to scrap in alleys when
I choose. Mother always said
I'd meet a sorry end.

Barbara Goldberg

MOORINGS

Because he picked up Newsweek and said,
"When you get your head together come
talk to me," and because seven years before
he didn't help me over the ice, I saw a lawyer.
I do not live in Sneed's Landing nor fly
in private planes. I am no longer
married to the man with the golden
American Express card. He said, "Don't
count on me," and at the end I didn't.
I moved. I remarried. I had two sons.
My husband says, "Count on me," while
counting on me. He says, "You have
a problem with femininity, you can't
trust men." All day he hears intimate
details of other lives. He comes home, says,
"Be warm, be loving, be mine." I am

safe harbor for children, friends, husbands.
Those who cruise upon me puff and strain, think
I am their own river. My thoughts sail
on a green couch. Adrift, memory washes me
back to Carlsbad, Berlin, Prague. I relive
lives in old photographs, anchored in sepia.

from WRITINGS FROM THE QUATTROCENTO

From the letters and journal entries of Tommasa di Benedetto Malefici, wife of Paolo Uccello, the Renaissance painter and sculptor. He considered his work on Perspective Theory to be of primary importance.

Journal entry, All Saints' Day, 1427

To him it is a game.
I could crack an egg, or
pull my hair, it's all
the same. He looks up
with a baffled mien
before returning with ardent
concentration to his compass
and protractor. He maps out
a multitude of intersecting
lines and shifts an angle here,
an angle there in the wild
hope that all lines
will meet in the infinite distance.
I know he wracks his brain —
how can the appearance of near
and far be rendered on a flat
plane? This intricate problem
absorbs him, keeps him young
and buoyant. When we dine
I feel his years fall upon me
in the candlelight. After soup
and fish and flan the lines
around my eyes and mouth define themselves
more deeply. If he raised his eyes
to really look at me, he'd see how near
and far are merely metaphor of present,
past and future. Ah, but his realm is space
and all its variations, while mine is time.
The two realms intersect of course: for instance,
when he went far, I ached for his return.

Now that he's here I feel a greater
distance. And when he strokes my breast
I know he thinks of orthogons and where
to plot the vanishing point. My Paolo
truly serves a higher Master. He does
not wish to scorn me. But I am young
to renounce the pleasures of the flesh, once
having known such mad trembling. I should be
grateful for his fidelity. He does not cast
an eye at other comely women. If only
I were an ordinary chalice to be analyzed!
He would view me with greater fascination,
and I would be held in dearer regard.

SONG WHILE ARRANGING JASMINE AND JEWELWEED

1

You ask me, when did it begin?
When I saw you at the mercado
sniffing a cantaloupe. Ramon!
The way you held that melon it must
have ripened in your hand. That night
in the ballroom, it was your sparkling
mustache, the pearl stud in your tie.
And when you entered me it was as though
you already knew me, so sure was your beat,
so emphatic my reply. Adorado! I told you
I had many lovers. You knew I lied.

2

When you give me that cock-
eyed, cross-eyed, pie-eyed
look, oh my pet, I know
you're feeling the itch
to travel. That's when
I stick a rose in my hair,
light a cigarillo and offer
to button your spanking white
shirt. Adios, Ramon, bye bye!
I shut the door with finesse
and greet my own heart, sweet
heart, faithful dumb pumper.

3

Take care where you plant your feet,
my Latin-American strongman.
There's a hot tarantella on the tip
of my tongue. Don't tell me to shut
my mouth — I say what I please.
And if there's an earthquake I get
the doorway. So there's a dead one

floating in the milk. A cockroach here
can be rocked in a cradle. I don't
wear these pointy shoes for nothing.
I am no dumb blonde you swept away.
I play my part with proper agitation.

4

It's Sunday, and here comes Ramon.
All is forgiven, my docile lambkin!
Let's bleat together under the covers.
Come nuzzle the pale globe of my belly,
come drink from my goblet of love.

NÉE MAGGIE MALONE

She didn't shave her legs or underarms
because her husband said it was unnatural
which is fine in Zagreb but in summer
heat at the Safeway she felt savage
like when she'd had to go in the middle of
the night at his family's farmhouse and relieved
herself in a pot which she hid in the closet.

That summer the pick-up died while he was restoring
houses on Capitol Hill for "that bastard Grodski
doesn't he know I'm craftsman   no bubbles when I
paint walls" and that summer Rudy still suckled at
Maggie's breast though he was four and her female
friends thought it bizarre even perverse.

What would they say if they knew he crawled nightly
into their bed wetting the sheets   Maggie
stumbling for the child's cot while father and son
slept on together.

Then he was fired by that bastard Grodski who said
he was arrogant and Maggie told friends he quit
because he couldn't take orders from a crook
who didn't appreciate fine work.

They were poorer next summer and he said, "Save money
make sheets" and she thought about it   then he said
"Be useful   learn Croatian" and he gave her a dictionary
and she tried in late afternoons to say the words
while the new baby nursed and Rudy clung monkey-like
to her furry legs.

Irish jigs played on the phonograph   she thought
I should make sheets   I should learn Croatian
she hummed the reels thinking   I'd like to
shuffle stomp stomp stomp shuffle stomp stomp stomp

CULTIVATED GROUND

Your father, perennially desirous
of a perfect lawn, always blamed
the shade, the soil, a laxness
of moral fiber for his failure.

Yours is a careful house:
tulips lie flat on percale,
pots are fitted with matching
lids, the piano is always in tune.

Seasonable nights you make a pilgrimage
to the front yard. Trowel in hand
you dig up encroaching weeds
before new seeds are released.

Beneath your layer of manicured
green, roots of pigweed, quack-
grass, cocklebur and teasel
nestle and creep.

COMING OF AGE

Dressed and coiffed and openly searching
for eyes of approval: enter my mother,
Loretta Young, sweeping dress into line,
her body attuned to each raised eyebrow,
her charming hauteur from another age.
And me, mouth agape, plucking

the hem of my skirt to cover my knees, plucking
up courage to untie my tongue, searching
for clever words, so clever for my age,
and if not artless, then cuter than mother
so my father behind the newspaper would show his eyebrow
and maybe even an eye to me (hardly next in line).

I'd be obvious, mimicking, out of line.
My older sister, fat, lugubrious, plucking
the specks of dust from her lap, furrowed eyebrow
downturned on books, the floor, searching
for ways to escape my coldly beautiful mother
who knew my sister would always be ugly; it wasn't just age.

And later, when blooming, I came of age
the boys long and gangly stood in line
and gazed enraptured first at my mother
till I came downstairs, plucking
a daisy, hoping, always searching
for proof of affection in an eyebrow.

Does he love me, does he not, for the eyebrow
behind the paper denied me, no matter the age.
No matter he died. I was fourteen, still searching
for the proper gesture, the exact line
to stop the endless critical plucking
at each imperfection. My mother

endured his erratic eruptions. My mother
knew by a flick of her wrist, a raised eyebrow
she could get him to bed, him plucking
the clothes from her body, she shedding years from his age.
We never had a chance, there was no line
to help my sister or me. We're still searching.

My mother before the mirror plucking
an eyebrow ruthlessly, searching
for lines of creeping age.

TEETH

We all live in dread of our teeth
falling out into our cupped palms.
We pray for our teeth, clattering
in the bone-chamber of the skull.
And when the little insanities
creep up from our throat, our teeth,
good soldiers holding their ground,
grind them down in our sleep. And praise
to the wolf with his sharp incisors,
the better to eat. And the ice-maiden's
teeth, sheathed in enamel, biting clean
through the bone. Oh we would never
depart from our eyeteeth, rooted dependably
above our unremarkable necks. And who
is not awed by the white buds of milkteeth
that sprout from red plushness and become
the cutting edge.

CAUTIONARY TALES

In the woods
are these things:

fingers of madmen
nimble and quick
playing cat's cradle
with ropes meant for strangling

a great horned owl
in a treetop
the soul of a Chippewa
caught in its throat

a sidewinding snake
rubbing its scales
jaws unhinged
hungry for neckbones

quicksand, though no one
knows where exactly
take care where your foot falls
for that's where your mouth fills

These are stories our children tell us
to keep us from wandering.

Elaine Reisler Magarrell

Elaine Magarrell

CLINTON, 1942

Mother made chicken soup.
Our bowls were ringed with gold.
They were wide as Mother's face
and our spoons dripped scalding broth.

As we ate, farmers loafed
in front of the store.
It was open for business.

Hitler screamed on the radio.
Mother sold a green coat
to a woman whose son
was the age to go.

That summer I minded the store
in a grasshopper storm.
Grasshoppers stuck to the windows
and drifted against the door.
I shoveled them into a sack like bones.

Elaine Magarrell

ON HOGBACK MOUNTAIN

The crickets are loving their legs,
the blue jay is being pestered by sparrows,
the mountain is sounding.
A snake got up like an argyle sock
crosses the trail.
I stick to my rock.
The snake loops out
like a Chinese buttonhole
just as a boulder lets go of the ridge
with a sound that picks up
all other sounds by the skin of their necks.
The whole tribe of noise shoves off
down the mountain for Boise.

It is more quiet than you can imagine.
The crickets, the blue jay, the sparrows, the snake
all are still.
My eyes are pinned closed by surprise.
It is the crickets who notice first
that they are all right.
Then the sparrows.
The jay isn't sure and the snake
buttons himself to a lichened knob.
I go to the edge of the ridge
and look over.

Elaine Magarrell

WET

It rains inside,
water rises two flights.
Outdoors the elm
trolls back and forth
catching at glass
in the window.

We wring out our lives,
tie a corner of yours
to mine and the bedpost,
throw them over the sill
and jump.
We land in Mexico

drunk. I wear red silk
in the morning
and sequined sneakers.
The water is up to our waists
and rising. You say
I am beautiful wet
and we share a bottle of beer
and a taco plate.

Red snappers kiss at my sneakers.
You dive in your
three-piece business suit,
come up with a fish
in your teeth.
It slaps at your bridgework.
I troll my shoes
in the stream.

GOOD GIRL

I know what a good girl is.
I have been a good girl,
flattered those who scorn me,
listened hours to a bore.
I do anything to please.
I shut my mouth,
feel guilty on demand.
I know what a good girl is.

I am such a good girl,
I dress up in a plain brown wrapper,
at parties I don't mix with men,
I would never kiss my doctor.
I know what a good girl is.

I will be a good girl,
smile until my mouth aches.
I will not tell the truth.
I will not tell the truth.

ZOLANA

Flatchested town along the Mississippi past McKenna Field,
no ticket needed to the county courthouse.
Slap the marble floors, rub your back along the cold red stones,
use the bathroom free.
You might see Zolana powdering her chin moles.

Zolana ran the counter at the courthouse cafeteria.
She was my friend when I was in fifth grade
and thought that only Jews got breasts.
That was the year I read *King's Row* with hands cross-cupped
against my chest in Zolana's living room.

We stood together naked for the front hall mirror,
she a woman fully, I becoming,
two models longing for a painter.

She touched my breasts
and spoke in thin anticipation of brassieres,
the tyranny of motherhood, the proud mouths of lovers.

Zolana, it is better than you said.

RODEO

Out of the gate of the womb
into the ring I ride
female.
I can do anything.
By the time I am five
I can lasso the cat,
lean over the hose to drink,
bring my wet chin to my sleeve
like a cowhand.
By seventeen I earn a good living
from the back of a horse
picking up handkerchiefs,
sweeping the dust with my teeth.

The slippers I wear in the paddock
are a gift from my daughter,
Carma Lu Ann
who plays harmonica in and around Chicago.
At thirty-two she is my youngest.
When she was four she played *Clair de Lune*
on rubberbands.

Once a year I meet Sid
at a club in Chicago where Carma Lu plays.
It is a shock seeing his face again,
feeling his hand on my neck,
having him ask me again if I'm ready
to settle in to a house in East Quincy.
I tell him the prizes I won
in Cheyenne.
We have a few beers and Carma Lu plays
"Chicago Rock Clair de Lune."

Elaine Magarrell

MRS. VENTURE ADVANCES

Mrs. Venture advances, holding her bric-a-brac bones
out to the sidewalk ice, betting her legs
on the three-buckle boots she bought in the blizzard of '50.
At the corner she mails to Vermont an order
for daffodil bulbs, then shuffles an inch at a time
to the drug store to sit at the counter.
She is friends with the counter girl, Hattie.
Mrs. Venture lives without cats in the house Henry bought
before he died. When they were children
they ran off together in spite of his mother.

Then her favorite grandson eloped
with an older woman, divorced from the mailman.
Dottie, her daughter, tried to protect her:
"Mama, he's gone joined the Navy.
He took his guitar picks and left."
Old Mrs. Venture turned toward the wall
where the cobwebs shook in the air from the heat vent.
She smelled a lie as quick as a fart in the closet.
"He'll be all right, Dottie," she said. "He's a good boy."

Elaine Magarrell

REFUSING THE EYE

Eye roots run deeper than roots of teeth.
Eyes branch on the palms of hands,
show beneath fingernails, walk on the tops of feet.
Each of the senses spends on the eye —
smell trades a breath of snow for the eye's ice crystal,
vectors of rose are gifts from a voice.

I became solely engaged in seeing.
I could see cells in human skin
as they moved. I could map exhalations of birds
in flight and discern the half-sweat
that precedes hesitation.
My friends avoided me.
Out of loneliness, I refused the eye,
relied on the interior sense of touch that is feeling.
Now withered roots of sight deprive me
of properly tasting and hearing.
No oranges rise from the moons of my nails
and my hands holding music could be handling newsprint.
Except for the flower ends of the organ
which faint behind lids,
there is nothing with which I can see.

Elaine Magarrell

LAST CHILD

After the fire
men lived on the desert,
women lived near the mountain
where there was shade.
All other land was flattened and melted.

Whatever was spared by the fire seemed holy.
Rosemary sprang from between the rocks on the mountain.
With its bruised leaves women perfumed the skin
of the last child on earth.

The child had seen miracles —
once a small bird.
She had seen stars
and color in water.

She was told by the women
that she would give birth to a child.
They taught her the way it is done.

When it was time, the man was a stranger.
He had come far for this
the old women told her.
They straightened her hair,
held on to her shoulders.

The man touched her body in places,
gathered the scent of rosemary
as though he, too, were a child.
The old women moaned; their eyes were open.

On the grey desert a mist arose
like a field of white iris.
From the bald mountain a mist descended.
Between the last child and the woman she was becoming
there was a clearing — a place of flowers.

Elaine Magarrell

WORDS HAVE SEX LIVES OF THEIR OWN

She undressed her words
so their bones would show
and joints would move
in unusual ways.
The words turned around,
they made love in her mouth.
What a coup for the language.
The chaste in the room
effervesced from their ears,
changed their minds
to erogenous zones.
Every sentence they spoke
knew a sensuous root,
every phrase
kept a sentence or two
on the side. Every word,
it was learned, had once squealed
with delight in the bed,
with delight in the bed of the mind.

Mariquita MacManus Mullan

Mariquita MacManus Mullan

STOPPED FOR A RED LIGHT: MIAMI

Where are you going, Thelma,
why do you wait on Flagler
and First as the angry sun
flames up in your auburn hair?
I can guess where you're from:
Grand Forks or Syracuse
where you had many admirers.
Do you have at least one
friend in this town?

You must have a lineage
old as the Everglades;
your elegant limbs
were prefigured in claws
on some scaly body,
and even loneliness
must have been known
in your ancestral cave
some time during the pleistocene.

Where are you going, Thelma,
in white shorts, spike heels,
hands on your hips?
I think you'd be missed
in some shuttered room
if you should sink down
and your beautiful curves
vanish into archaic sands
shifting around
beneath Flagler Street.

HEIRESS

I live inside
my life as I live
within the walls
of the house
I have inherited,
mistress of bleached
and pleated curtains,
abundant dark brocade
and an established
line of thought.

I rearrange opinions
in the way I change
the velvet chairs.
Crafted long ago,
they will never need replacement.
Ideas, like still-lifes
on the wall,
preserved with care
are rarely moved.

I am never seen
to walk beyond the plot
where hollyhocks
resign themselves
along the iron fence
nor turn to take
a long view of the house
nor speculate on
traveling abroad.

Mariquita MacManus Mullan

INCIDENT AT DOW

The gulls it seems were exiled from the delta
when oil spilled on their hot and gritty coast.
They landed on a factory parking lot
where tender-hearted workers turned from toxic vats
to scatter sand and shells across the glistening tar
which made a kind of beach for nervous birds
and cheered the workers at their routine tasks.

LAMENT FOR THE BULL

("*Eran las cinco en punto de la tarde*"
from Lament for Ignacio Sanchez Mejias, the bullfighter
—Federico Garcia Lorca)

What was the truth of the happening:
who were you who stood your ground
while the giant muscle in your back
was skewered by picadors?
Who were the two whose destinies merged
at five o'clock in the afternoon?

Across the ring he poised on toe,
in his blue suit of lights,
ran in with the banderillas
and slung them beyond your startled eyes,
pinned them, swaying, into your neck
at five o'clock in the afternoon.

You disdained the crimson cape
as he taunted you
and passed with grace,
stood firm then struck;
the sword slid deep behind your horns
at five o'clock in the afternoon.

Was it for this you were nurtured
on the plains of Estremadura?
You shivered, gathered your final
ton of terrible force and charged,
gave him the horn, hurled
a trajectory blue and crimson
arching across the sand
at five o'clock in the afternoon.

They bore him away with honor
amid the roar of lament.
No honor for you
as they dragged you
in dust and blood from the ring
your blackness crushing
sunbeams to death
at five o'clock in the afternoon.

MIRAGE

Up on the bath-house wall
hands of the giant clock
close in on time,
try to contain it.

The glass dome sealed
to a hot stone wall
contemplates the day,
and green noonshade

of palms on dune grass,
red umbrellas and bathers
in the shimmering distance.

But the long hour trickles
past dripping showerheads
down half-wet stone
escapes across the sand

past umbrellas,
past the graceful bending forms
slides into ocean's careless frill
in glittering slanted lines.

Mariquita MacManus Mullan

THE PROFESSOR

He wanders to the post box down the way
his old tweed hangs like burlap to the knees
and reeks of pencils, pipes and mildewed cheese —
no editor has sent good news today.
The aging bloodshot eyes take on a glaze
of resignation, but with smiles he greets
the neighbors' children, lets them search for sweets
in pockets jammed with notes for epic plays,
scraps of poems, old clips of critics' praise.
He'd walked among the lions, brushed by fame.

One letter starts: "We're honoring your name . . ."
he'd be *Emeritus* in several days.
Though lanterns light behind the hazy eyes
there's neither disappointment nor surprise.

ASPECTS OF THE CITY

DOWNTOWN

Indifferent mirrors of the city
four glass faces of this building
gaze toward compass points.
Spines of bronze run
from spire to street —
giant zippers if undone
could bring this tower down
unfolding like a concrete
flower with square petals.

WEST SIDE

In Kaplan's Dairy Restaurant,
windows steam
from chicken soup and kreplach,
the waitress juggles
bowls of borscht, inquires
"Dolling, this your soup? Look
is missing from this table
sugar bowl. Now who
is taking home yet
sugar bowls?"

UPPER EAST SIDE

On Madison Avenue
ghosts in picture hats
and hobble skirts
descend the stoops
and stroll unseen
among the galleries.
One hot day in 1910
an overburdened dray horse
pulling the ice cart
flopped down here and died.
Brownstones locked
in tight embrace;
their smoky windows frown
on pavements hiding
cobbles buried far beneath.

WEATHER REPORT

Drizzle in Ho Chi Minh City
Cloud covers Toulouse . . .

Here by the Park the blowing March rain
forces premature dogwood blossoms
to whirl from the trees.
Wind sends a message —
spring already a herald of fall.

Snowing in Moscow today
Clear skies in Des Moines . . .

Passing among the umbrellas
by Tiffany's clock
your marvellous face appears
for a moment, bewitching
smiling at someone
not seeing me.

Precipitation in Dallas and Paris
Sunny in Rome
Local forecast: chilly and fog . . .

SUNDAY MORNING 4 a.m.

I take the measure of the city:
aloof but not indifferent.
Light blooms in yellow flowers
on rainy streets
glows on a canopy of fog.
Am I the only one to hear
the moan of a tugboat,
the click of a traffic light
switching from red to green
on the empty avenue,
the sound of one horn blowing?

PLANE TREE

A city tree of common origin and double roots
flourished tough, assertive in a stony yard
leaned densely against my sixth-floor windows
threw spare shadows on the blinds in winter
swung wildly at the panes in summer storms
filtered light to rows of households down below
and spread green shade across a neighborhood of roofs.
The tree was crowded like the neighborhood,
a gathering place for bickering black squirrels
and several autocratic cardinals.

At dawn I flip the blinds — the tree is gone.
The outlook is uncompromising: cubes
of brick or black and white. Lost
in the geometry of chimneys
and multilevel flats, cardinals no longer
streak across the window, squirrels
disdain the butchered stump
and scramble off to farther streets.
The tree, an afterimage on my memory, is real
as an amputated limb that still gives pain.
I hear the distant questions of the birds.

Mariquita MacManus Mullan

MEMORIAL DAY ON OMAHA BEACH

In his lap is a camera;
the man in white pants
rolls past the crosses
looking for friends.
Left on the Beach
with no legs, he lived.
Those who left him
lie under crosses.
So he goes, wondering,
on wheels.

Elisavietta Ritchie

Elisavietta Ritchie

PROPITIATIONS

She leaves one apple for the orchard elves
so next fall's crop will overflow.

One daisy clump survives her scythe.
And of her splashing catch, the fish

who speaks she throws back to the sea
to grant three wishes in return for life.

She places bowls of milk out every night
for black snakes, cats and salamanders,

and caters crumbs for spirits as for birds.
She rings the house with daffodils

and shelters all her babies anxiously.
But she knows: the fairest is the one they'll claim.

Among her lovers, also one must be
abandoned to ensure the rest.

THE GYPSY IS SUMMONED BEFORE THE MILITIA

Your questions I don't understand,
but the word "interrogation" embraces
pages of terror . . . I know no names.

In the past, those who questioned me
sought information only on themselves.
I know nothing about anyone till he asks.

Then I see through hill and cloud and skin and skull,
trace seines of lines and lives . . . And lies.
I never forget a hand . . . I know no names.

I hold the seed of half of Europe in my womb.
My gypsy babes will steal across the earth.
I know no names.

I've gleaned the pain of millions. Yes,
I fear the gleam of your instruments.
I know no names.

Look, I am old, and my purple skirts
are dank from your jail.
My silver has tarnished. You've stolen my gold.

But my hair remains long and black.
My legs stay slim from dancing to tambourines.
I could show you a good time.

Come, dismiss those surly guards at the doors.
Tear up your reports. Outside these walls
a caravan is waiting for us.

I could reveal the future of your regime.
I'd read your own fortune, free.
Come along . . . I can tell you now:

The lines on my palm
are longer than yours.
And I know your name.

FOR A CERTAIN SLAVIC NOVELIST

Some are jailed,
or expelled, or killed.

You exile into yourself,
to wander, a stranger learning

the language of madness.
You forge an alien passport

to prove yourself
at the common border of sanity.

They search the elegant luggage
you invent for the trip,

but insanity does not appear
contraband in that land,

paranoia is ordinary as
your dressing gown spotted with omelette.

Any odor of espionage
is masked by the sticky elixir

which leaks from the half-screwed
bottlecap of your brain.

Farewell, and safe journey.
Someday it may be safe to return.

   * * * * * * * * *

Post Scriptum: June. Then why,
when you finally came back,

were you pushed from the window?
Or did you really jump?

Elisavietta Ritchie

IN THE ARCHIVES

Frayed books, scratchy maps of half-baked campaigns,
browned photos of soldiers with antique rifles
defending the mud of the trenches,
visiting princes inspecting the cannons,
anonymous prisoners slogging through towns
with unpronounceable names . . .

Suddenly: my grandfather's photograph!
He is the new governor general of captured Galicia.
He stands before the Czar's portrait
wearing his gallery of medals.
His moustache has been trimmed for the picture,
and the dust of battles scraped from his boots.

He has shown his love for the troops,
his concern for prisoners and refugees,
won the respect of the foe, some envy from peers.
He has fought a number of losing battles
and survived a court martial with honor.
He is brilliant, foolish, on good terms with God.

He stands very straight. It is 1915.
He will not govern for long.
But both sons will uphold the family name
on several battlefields.
One will die fighting with valor.
The other, though wounded, will recover in exile.

Grandfather will stay, through war, revolution,
prison, banishment, famine, to die
of malnutrition and a tired heart.
The books recording his deeds will be lost
or banned, or revived and the facts distorted.
Nor is it sure how well he will live in the archives.

Elisavietta Ritchie

MY FATHER, COLONEL, U.S. ARMY, RETIRED

The shell explodes and scatters light
and alien fingerbones. He isn't sure
if this is real or dream,
but screams until he wakes.
The household wakens also, terrified.
He is embarrassed, and confused,
thinks he's back at Anzio, Monte Cassino,
Normandy, the Battle of the Bulge.
Though forty years have passed, the war
goes on, and shrapnel, rubble and
peculiar shards of flesh
still litter all the bedroom floor so deep
he cannot find his slippers in the dark.

SISTERHOOD

Beneath the palms of Marrakesh
my bastard half-sister survives, I think . . .

Our travelled father told me of
his long-ago adventure.
Sometimes I wonder if
he's wondering, as he stares at me:
Does she share our blue eyes and carrot hair?
Or was her dusky mother dominant?

Has she, in turn, borne throw-back babes —
thrust in trash heaps outside city gates
before they breathed too deeply of the desert air
and shocked her tribe with carrot hair, blue eyes?

Still, her mother let her live,
embarrassing or cherished legacy,
though that unlettered lovely Moorish maid
found new employers and new loves
when Daddy travelled on . . .

My sister, are you leading revolutions, or
a herd of donkeys to the waterhole?

Elisavietta Ritchie

HOMECOMING FROM INDONESIA

You drew me a map for my journey,
inked rivers and coastlines in blue,
crayoned valleys and paddies green,
mountains you pencilled brown,
designed volcanos with red,
noted meteorological facts
and storm warnings black.

I return having learned
geographies you would not teach,
the fragrance of frangipani
sketched in my hair,
the taste of unusual fruit
mapped on my lips,
others' embraces charting
my skin you find foreign.

I bring you saffron umbrellas
tasselled with bells,
baskets of silver and silk,
the chiming of gamelans, gongs
and flutes to shatter your silence,
warm waterfalls, black butterflies,
and feathers from finches stabbed
to honor a masked demi-god.

Yet you, who sent me forth to explore,
blockade your ice-bound harbor against
my cargo of treasures.
From offshore I can see
our old terrain's out of tilt,
familiar valleys upheaved,
new cliffs too steep to scale . . .
My return was the journey away.

THE NANTUCKET WHALER'S LADY

This brick house wobbles on a bed of sand.
How rickety my widow's walk above
those beige cobblestones. The next hurricane
could topple us into Nantucket Sound.
Through storms and fogs and sunny days I search
for one sight of your sail.

You search the warmer China Seas for spouts
and cinnamon and tea — or silken girls
in Surabaya, Hong Kong, Singapore
and intermediate ports of recall.
Unless your harpoon miss, your craft capsize,
you might return next year.

But I'm tired of tatting and keeping watch,
and bored with breasting your bastards. Give me
the lusty butcher who pursues the sheep
on graygreen moors, or the local tanner,
his hands, till they touch my hide, barely washed
of the blood of the goat.

None of your sweet "But I've brought you baleen
for your corset, my love!" My waist remains
hourglass, as if to mark the sands of
your absence. Your gifts of silk may become
my shroud . . . And don't ship home any more bones:
I've scrimshaw enough.

What matter if blubber glows in my lamp
through lonely winters dim with mist and snow,
and summer evenings fragrant with privet, fig,
wild rose, honeysuckle and mackerel.
No match for your light, your settings on fire.
I want conflagrations.

So hang a flotilla of riding lights
high up your mast, and come back, Captain Jack,
or whatever I called you years ago
when you set your seven sails and cast off
with a running tide and the slippery
excuse of chasing whales.

106

LEARNING TO KEEP A LOW PROFILE

*Upon reading in a New York Times ad
that the CIA offers "opportunities"*

Opportunistically now I'll begin
my overdue training in anonymity:

I'll hide my notorious red hair
in turbans preserved from the '30s,

my eulogized eyes and strawberry lashes
behind smoky glasses,

my Akhmatovian nose
in a book, veil or muffler.

My insignificant breasts
should cause no disturbance,

but at your signal I'll wiggle my hips.
My fingers will leave only dubious prints.

I'll choose assumed names
of indefinite source, ambiguous orthography.

My accents will multiply,
illegible signatures vary.

I'll board unregistered ships
for undisclosed ports,

flash passports from outlandish states.
Shifty, elusive, mysterious,

I'll slither through corridors foreign
while ignoring familiar eyes.

No champagne. Soda in shabby cafes
on streets whose names change with each coup,

while I pursue international affairs
with small and balding Hungarians

in bankrupt mineral spas.
No one will decipher my codes.

Nor will I write books or give interviews
till the time I choose to tell all.

CHOREOGRAPHY

Not at the far side of the music but
caught in the vortex now
everything is mystery, surprise

I'm captured in a dance
not yet prefigured
and pattern unpredictable

I can't forehear the notes
and only know
they're new and intricate

But may they score
a graceful culmination
to this life of stumbling steps

Elizabeth Sullam

CLARITY OVER THE ADRIATIC

Early September in the afternoon
clarity flows from sky to sea to eyes
then again from eyes to sea to sky.

It is as though light-soaked hours
imbue the steel-glazed glare of the sea and —
in time so short that it's no time at all —
flare into the countless pathways of my brain,
through neurons and synapses that perceive
that glowing brightness, boundless, undefined,
and send no sharp reply. In the same while

the hubbub of the beach draws farther,
colors pale, shapes lose boundaries,
and the body, dispossessed of flesh, is
taken on a backward journey into
the moment when a vast radiance first
appeared, just before space darkened,
matter spun, and time rushed in.

MISERERE

Hours of hills, barren ravines,
chancy tablelands, run behind bodies
like springs wrung, and released by flight.
Breath beats the heart on shell-shocked leaves,
any beat last-ticking. Feet crash undergrowth.
Hands, clutching weapons, push aside
anything lying in the corrupted woods.
Pupils dilated by faces of death
telescope fragments of sky,
scarlet announcements of dark.
Miserere for the foe, ally of few decades ago.

* * * * * * * *

Hours of hills behind, bodies tense
and relax in pursuit. Hands grip weapons,
hold steering wheels, adjust sights
over the hills ahead. Feet tread trails
the enemy has trod.
Death-filled eyes probe clearings,
scan the same sky
for comforting signs of night.
Miserere for the ally, our future enemy.

* * * * * * * *

Night, be dark over the shaken hills.
Hills, be cave-scooped, steep-walled,
cloud-capped, hide shadow-casting moons.
The parsley flower and rosemary wither.
Glowworms dim on your scorched skin.
Miserere for those who will not see dawn.

* * * * * * * *

Lower all flags. They fly colors of death.
In eerie wind they swirl and spin and twist
the insane blazon of Cain.
Miserere for the mother who will curse her womb.

* * * * * * * *

Bards, cover your mouths. Take a good look.
We do not die for glory. Where we are going
even glory rots. Hear the screams jetting forth.
See the blood clotted by terror, cratered hearts,
charred flesh, gushing entrails, the anguished masks
fleeting before darkness sucks us in. *Miserere,*
miserere for all herds driven to stockyards.

MINE-FIELD — 1946

Horns of black bulls
on the rim of the sun.
Shadows of crows
fly left
through sulfur skies.
The ace of spades
turned upside down.

Within dark steel seeds
a blind core ticks,
waits in rows,
under the sleepless
vipers of the grass.

A ball, heavy with cold air
and raven breath, moves
along the path
of broken columns.

Where are you going, child,
with your hands
full of wind and
feet full of wings?

Sweet oleander
of unlucky womb
black wind splinters
ripped you away,
long tongues of purple flames
charred your petals.

Sweet oleander
of parched night,
the half-closed door
of your mother house
is draped by hearts
burned black
and the foam
of crystal tears.

114

AUGUST NIGHT IN THE EMILIAN LOWLANDS

Poplars of fireflies
and falling stars
crown Etruscan canals
and ambush the silence.

Willows of witchcraft
and watermagic trace
Roman land-divisions
over Gallic defeat.

Silky Chinese foam
rises on mulberry leaves
and the moon grows richer
with white fruits
in the obsidian night.

In Byzantine cloisters,
moonridden, stray dogs
wail the sorrow
of the absent Jews.

An immense poppy closes,
bonfires burn
on multiple horizons.

Within flatland cages
of canes and dry-wheat breezes,
cicadas, nightingales and toads
scythe their sickle-songs
and harvest the spikes of silence.

LEAVING

It was hard to leave the house,
the misty river and stones
that hold so much of one
and those who came before,
and made all bear
their space, their heaviness and air.

To open gates, tear down walls,
go outside and understand
the winds of the plains;
to reach the river mouths and feel
what rivers feel when
their sweet waters meet
the salty waters of the sea;
to cross straits, be at the merge
of sea with ocean; stand where
oceans, drinking distant sands
and rocks, are drunk by them;
to follow spice routes and
the bargaining of souls and gods;
learn the tongue of tongues,
and seek the bluest flower.
This is an act that must be done
to reconcile that part of one
that wants to be what one is not
and free.

Joy of breaking loose —
only to feel the stones have grown
heavier on one's shoulders, wells deepened,
and find winds blow only
silence on the plains,
oceans swallow sweet waters
and drown seafarers;
great routes crumble into ruins;
spices dry and souls are sold into slavery;
gods fight over nothing;
blue flowers do not bloom;

and one is always crouched
in secret gardens,
watching the same fountains,
where the nightingale
is mad with night,
and blood with jasmine
and nightshade,
where one grows to be
what one becomes.

Elizabeth Sullam

YOU NO LONGER SAIL THE BOAT

She lies upon the shore
of our pine-walled cove.
The current steers, at whim,
the helm unlashed,
the hull long thrashed
by wind and wave, the name washed out.
You no longer name me mate.

At night, at the Casino,
the roulette wheel
swivels against my bet.
No more chips are left.
You don't sound out the spinnings,
other games lure you, dark
games I don't yet know.

You don't see me returning to the dock.
The breakers churn and foam. Our boat
surges, like a figment of herself,
chiseled, waiting
against the flares of the sky,
and does not know my coming and going.

The footsteps sandaled
in the needles of the sloping lane
through the pine grove, sag into silence.
You now walk other paths, unknowing . . . .

and here, in the last slice of my evening
listening for your laughter,
I keep hearing only the sea.

CONFLUENCE

for Bosa De Franceski

Someone, I have forgotten who,
used to say we make friends
only in childhood, Bosa,
and I thought so too, till our Sunday
afternoon stroll along the Sava,
that carried far away tales and
suggestions of spring into the Danube.
We too merged the unique times of two women,
no matter how middle-aged, an intimate
confluence. Like the rivers, Bosa,
we are travellers of great distances,
nothing too short or too long for our course.
Our religion is the law of flowing,
in time of great clouds or terse skies,
digging and filling our space.
Our temptation is the plain, our sin is
outflowing, our redemption receding,
our interdict the rock, our passion the sea.
We keep flowing forth, mindless of
unsteady earth below, of men's tales,
and surreal time-space, searching for
affinity, which is the confluence
of elements composing and composed . . .
At the frown of the land we wash,
we wash the brown salt on the banks
with spiced waters, feeding
rosemary, myrtle and linden,
leaving scented driftwood
at the gates of men's cities.
We are women of a new fauna,
not guilty or innocent,
outside the Bible and the Koran,
women of ourselves, nobody else's.
The sum of our flowing has come together
in the same breath of wind
carrying whiffs of emerald sea salts . . .
We are ready for the taste.
Our faces are not made up and wear no mask,
our hands still grip the scimitar
of the moon over low-flying birds of prey.

Elizabeth Sullam

BLACK CEMETERY IN GEORGETOWN

For Dr. Lee Eiden who on a misty day stroll
gave me the idea of "a graveyard of a graveyard".

The trees here float with winter mist,
ghosts strolling on soft shores.
Here, like is known by like
and contemplation is the contemplated.

A swollen river overflows.
Here, past spills over future and,
retreating, leaves the landscape changed.
Heaviness may levitate in mats
of gossamer, and veer to liquid syllables.
Mist, names, and gravestones meld
till they are one.

Read names on upright stones,
names that should have bloomed
like any flower in any season.
Instead, flowers bloom inward,
become the unintelligible change.

Within this shapeless graveyard
of a graveyard other somber changes
creep with larvae beneath the shell
of earth. Shorter than our dreams,
the images of death will live less than letters
chiseled on our fallen stones.

Even future quiescence is denied us.
We are not allowed to rest
in the calm prison of the trees;
nor the leaves, wise with what lies
between wind and absence of wind, are left
to draw the light, to us forbidden.

At the gate bulldozers wait to drag
marble, trees, earth and bones
to another stifling night.
A whiff of fog, perhaps
our last fighting breath,
will trespass over Oak Hill's
metal fences, to recall our alikeness,
the center of design
where spheres, opposites, and rules
come to their point of winter.

Margaret Weaver

Margaret Weaver

THE HAWK

A soft morning. Crossing the pasture
we startle shadows in and out of sight.
Mist like bright eyes floats silver in our hair.
It drops from close-preened pine needles like rain.

We walk in the grey air, hands clasped.
Then into our silence
crashes a red-tailed hawk.
Feathers fall, blood-stained; as he flies away
leaves shiver into place and the sun burns through.

So even the hawk's hunger opens to light.
Tonight we'll drink wine, talk till the oil lamp dims,
listen to the rustling in the eaves —
only this roof between us and the hawk's night.

Margaret Weaver

LULLABY

Under the sea, light falls and fades.
Water, stone and plant are shadows.
Green eddies lift weed fronds and let them
drop again in their slow wake.

Fish nose through intricate ways
among the trees. Beneath them,
our bones lie almost covered
by heavy, shifting sands, far from

other countries that we knew.
Through our rib branches, currents
in watery silence wash us
clean of flesh. We feed the creatures

who make our bones their home.
We hear no thunder. Lightning
tears the sea and touches us,
but we see nothing, nor fear its fire.

Cupped in our eyes, crabs
hum their sweet small songs of sleep.

ORANGE

An orange globe
cratered
a world in itself
with two poles
spins in a spiral
of carved peel.

Its skin spurts
oil droplets
sharp, pungent.

Crescent moons
spill from the center
into new orbits.

Spheres of juice
explode from the pores
and one seed, green-tipped
waits for creation.

STRANDED WHALES

Aground in shallows here, the dark whales lie
Beyond their limits, monstrous and serene.
Beneath the breezes and the sunny sky,
They face high silent dunes and land unseen,
Almost unmoving now. Their skin fades grey
As tide falls and wind dries flesh and sand.
Their wave-borne grace diminishes to sway
Of fins and flukes. They're alien to the end.

Although their eyes reflect us as they die,
We cannot understand what makes them dare.
Refusing the tide's pull, they seem to try
To change the natural laws of blood and air.
Still, in our common pulse, we feel the curl,
The sigh, of waves, and recognize our single world.

Margaret Weaver

THE SHADOW CATCHER

For Bruce Pierce

Elusive shadows sketch the desert walls
as clouds fly over, blown by high dry winds.
The painter tries to catch them as they fall

with tempera, with chalk or charcoal—all
contrive to keep the shadows from his hand
as rippling darkness lights the limestone walls.

Close to his hand, a spiny cactus sprawls.
Its long arms scatter shadows on the sand.
The artist seeks their likeness as they fall.

A horned skull white with shadow opens jaws,
and near the bones, quick grasses green the land.
A flickering shadow climbs the pale rock walls.

Though grey stones in the river bed recall
old storms, arroyos rarely know real rain.
The dreamer catching shadows feels it fall.

And if he caught them, could he keep them all?
Or would they fade? What is a shadow's end?
Elusive shadows climb the desert walls.
The painter brushes light as darkness falls.

REVENANT

From the green depths
   of the antique mirror,
from the bees and clover
   of its painted frame,
a face swims up,
   dark, weed-covered.

Ripples shatter it
   into hundreds
which surface, waver
   forward to sunlight.
Low banks and meadows
   of seeding grass
hold back the flood.

   If I touch the glass,
what will flow through my hand?

Margaret Weaver

UNDER WATER

Rain thickens the air. Leaves
slap wet against the window.
Gills remember how to breathe.

I see a robin float by
with hatching eggs. Her young
struggle from nest to water,
swim in a line like ducks
behind their mother.
Jays with outspread wings
scold the squirrels who splash
in the ivy border.
The neighbor's tortoise cat
follows the robins,
but they're safe by the big beech
beyond her depth. Bells jangle
and she turns to paddle back.

When the rain is over,
the squirrels find acorns
floated out of their holes.
The cat grooms her fur,
looks at the robins flying.
Gills close as the air dries.

Margaret Weaver

THE HOUSE MOVER

All landmarks missing,
the house moves on another plane,
backs and turns down narrow streets
lined with pale faces waiting under street lamps.
It bears secrets, old razor blades,
crows balanced on the roof.

Strained and scraped through the white city,
dropping shingles, shoes and packs of cards,
tearing off cobweb rags to blow in the wind,
the house leans around corners,
spills crickets to the road.
The crows peer down, flapping wings
disordered by the wind. Snow deepens.

Winds whirl by uncurtained windows,
sweep color and children's voices out the cracks.
Mirrors fall, chairs slide across the floor,
the kitchen boiler breaks its iron bands
and bounces away down an alley,
banging from wall to wall.

With day, the shards of mirrors swallow dark.
Now scoured clean, the house slips into place,
pulls its gardens close and gathers trees.
The crows regain their balance,
settle feathers, sleep.

Margaret Weaver

THE VINEYARD

We take the long view from winter.
Cold in the quiet, we remember
sun distilling sweetness in our veins.

On the south-facing hills,
terraced and staffed with vines,
looking down to distant farms,

we live again with warm rains,
the growing season and the green,
close in the swelling cluster

on one stem, hard, pale, red
or night blue with delicate bloom,
ripe for the harvest. We watch

the foxes spoil the vines,
birds quarrel over single grapes,
men carry off the vintage.

We remain, stem-bound to strangers,
darker, smaller, dryer
as day succeeds day and frost hardens.

When the stem breaks, we fall
alone, and in rich soil
beneath the vine, lie silent.

Margaret Weaver

COLLECTED FAIRY TALES

The old tales end well.
The frightened girl runs home.
The disenchanted prince and princess
live happy ever after. The third pig
resides in Georgian brick,
and on the book's cover,
takes a Sunday walk in his garden.
Here the giant's wife roasts whole oxen
and roving Jacks hide safe in her kitchen.

But the tales are not complete.
Years later, I learn
how the bears fear Goldilocks' story
and move to a new place
with an unlisted number;
how the charming princess, bored,
attempts real magic:
she kisses stones beside the well
and waits to see them move.
Her changed prince returns at night
to the marsh under the castle walls.

In the shadows
behind the cheerful pictures,
does the giant still fee fi fo
for human blood and bones?

CONTRIBUTORS' NOTES

E. CASTENDYK BRIEFS: Hawaii-born. Punahou, Scripps College, M.A. from Georgetown University. Translated German popular theology including Romano Guardini's *The Lord*, anthropological works on Hawaiian folk tales, and poetry by Rilke, Bachmann, Kirsch and the Comtesse de Noailles. Poems and translations in *The New Yorker, Saturday Review, Christian Science Monitor, The Journal of Literary Translation, Visions*, and *The American Poetry Anthology*.

MAXINE COMBS: Ph.D. University of Oregon; dissertation on The Black Mountain Poets. Taught English courses at American University, George Washington University, George Mason University, Idaho State University, Lane Community College and University of The District of Columbia. Reviews in *Poet Lore, Washington Times, Columbia Road Review, Northwest Review, Washington Review, Gargoyle* and *The Far Point*. Poems in *Whose Woods These Are, Piedmont Review* and others.

LUCIA DUNHAM: BA in Bacteriology, Smith College. Several awards in intercollegiate poetry contests. MD, University of Chicago. Was a Medical Officer at the National Institutes of Health in Bethesda, specializing in cancer research. Articles in *American Journal of Public Health, Acta Unio Contra Cancrum, Cancer Research, International Development Review, British Journal of Cancer* and other publications.

ELIZABETH FOLLIN-JONES: BA in Mathematics, University of Michigan. Sculptor now working in outdoor site-specific installations; sometimes uses poetry to complement her work. Poems and short prose accepted by *Washington Post, Christian Science Monitor, Poetry Review, Operative*, and others.

BARBARA HEYMANN GOLDBERG: BA in philosophy, Mount Holyoke. M.Ed. Columbia University. MFA program, American University. Taught in East Harlem and George Washington University. Wrote Harry Reasoner's radio commentaries at CBS. The Word Works Washington Prize 1982. Finalist, Pablo Neruda Poetry Contest. Poems and translations in *Poetry, Poetry Now, New England Review, Porch, Women in Therapy, Nimrod* and others.

ELAINE REISLER MAGARRELL: BA, English, University of Iowa, Graduate work in education at Drake University. Taught middle grade English in West Des Moines, Iowa and Iowa City, Iowa. Library clerk and researcher for the *New York Times* Washington Bureau. Free lance journalist. Published in *K-eight, Harper's, The Des Moines Register, Visions, Valhalla 8, English Journal* and *Poet Lore*.

MARIQUITA MACMANUS MULLAN: Studied creative writing at Columbia. BA in English and Spanish literatures from City University of New York. Published fiction and children's stories. Poems appear in *Christian Science Monitor, Piedmont Literary Review, The Archer/Camas Press*, the anthology *Whose Woods These Are*, and others. Awards from The Poetry Society of Virginia and National League of American Penwomen.

ELISAVIETTA ARTAMONOFF RITCHIE: Studied at Sorbonne, Cornell and Georgetown universities. BA, University of California, Berkeley, in English, French and Russian. MA, French literature, American University. *Tightening The Circle Over Eel Country* won Great Lakes Colleges' Association's "New Writer's Award For Best First Book of Poetry 1975-76." *Raking The Snow* won Washington Writers' Publishing House competition. Four chapbooks. Two annual awards, Poetry Society of America. Story selected by PEN/NEA Syndicated Fiction Project. Poems, stories, articles and translations in *New York Times, Washington Post, Christian Science Monitor, New Republic, National Geographic* and many other general and literary publications.

ELIZABETH SULLAM: Born and educated in Italy. Published in *Dossier* and *Federal Poets*.

MARGARET WEAVER: BA in History and Literature, Radcliffe College. M.Ed., George Washington University. Teaches in Maryland, tree-farms in Maine. Poems in *Yankee, Visions, Poet Lore, Passages North, Kyriokos, Kavitha* and others.